Colton Johnson has successfully buried the crazy attraction he feels for his younger stepbrother for so long, he can pretend he's not attracted to Asher at all. Graduating and dealing with the daily chore that is his bipolar disorder are the only two things on his mind. Then Colton makes the impulsive decision to accept his stepmother's invitation to visit. What Colton doesn't know is that Asher has been making plans.

With boundless enthusiasm, good looks, and endless amounts of persistence Asher Miller usually gets what he wants. The one plan that hasn't worked out for him is falling in love. He never thought his off limits, damaged, hot-as-sin stepbrother would be the one to catch his heart. For years Asher has squashed down his forbidden desire but now he's eighteen, he's following Colton's footsteps to college… and all bets are off. It's time to take the steps that will seduce Colton into love.

Step Into Love
Copyright © 2018 Lili Draguer
ISBN: 978-1-4874-2097-0
Cover art by Latricia Waters

Published by eXtasy Books Inc or
Devine Destinies, an imprint of eXtasy Books Inc
Look for us online at:
www.eXtasybooks.com or www.devinedestinies.com

STEP INTO LOVE
TABOO LOVE BOOK 2

BY

LILI DRAGUER

DEDICATION

For all the amazing lovers who are brave enough to take that step into love, especially when they have to walk through the dark days.

CHAPTER ONE

The fat, fluffy pillow came out of nowhere, hitting Colton in the side of the head and sending him sprawling sideways.

He was up again in half a second, arms raised and ready to fight. Eyes narrowed, leaning forward, he grabbed the pillow off the floor and held it cocked, ready to retaliate. *I just wanted to watch my show! In peace.* Colton scanned the room, ready to launch.

The only other person there was Asher, who was sitting in the tatty old brown chair across the room. The chair which used to have a large, decorative pillow on it. A blanket of warm yellow light draped Asher from a standing lamp. Otherwise, the living room was in evening shadow.

"Asher," Colton said sternly. The pillow was still raised, in case he decided to throw it.

Asher looked over, all wide-eyed innocence, but the tight press of his lips together to hide a smile gave it away.

"What the hell, Ash? I'm watching my show. What was that for?" Colton sagged back into the couch and let the pillow flop to the floor. No point in hitting Asher with it, not when he knew it was coming.

Asher shrugged. Colton flicked his eyes back towards the TV, quickly. *Does every move he makes have to look so good? Can't he be awkward just once? After ten freaking years I should be able to block him out but it's so hard when he looks amazing just shrugging.* Colton snuck another peek across the room.

Asher caught him looking, and there was a definite smile

1

in those melting brown eyes. "Sorry. Just felt like it." A tiny dimple next to his full lips appeared, making it so obvious he wasn't sorry. "This show is boring. Let's go do something. Get some pizza at Ralphio's. You can buy me a beer." Like always, Asher seemed poised to move, even sitting still in a chair. His fingers danced along the armrests, tapping out a rhythm with no beat, while his feet shifted along.

"And get hauled in to explain to the cops why I was supplying a minor? No." Colton turned back to the TV. Again. He tilted his chin and crossed his legs.

No, he didn't want to be alone for long periods of time with a distractingly hot younger man. No, he didn't want to admit he was avoiding it, either. Safer to sit here and watch the show, even though he had just lost the entire train of the plot.

Asher sighed and stood. Blue jeans hugged those lean hips and the dark gray cotton shirt clung to the muscles on his chest.

Maybe he'll take off by himself. Go away, Asher, and take those perfect pecs with you. Characters were arguing in the show. Something intense was going on. Fifteen minutes ago he had known what the plot was about. He uncrossed his legs and thought about heading up to his room.

The guest room he was staying in was nothing like his teeny little apartment near the campus. Nothing was left in it to show it had been his all through middle and high school, not one poster, or even the random wires and bits left from his home-built computer projects. Now it looked like it had been lifted straight from a nice, clean, slightly out-of-date hotel.

The cushions next to him shifted and he caught a whiff of a spicy soap smell as Asher sat. He knew it was Asher's shampoo because they had to take turns with the upstairs bathroom when he stayed here, and the whole hall burst with scented steam after one of his long showers. It wasn't like he used the soap himself. Off-brand dandruff shampoo was Colton's time-tested favorite. Not fancy musky stuff.

Asher slid across the couch, coming closer. Colton shifted away. Keeping at least six inches of space between them was an old, old habit by now.

Why did I want to visit this week? Pam and Dad have been divorced for a year now. I know *better than to put myself near Asher.* No one slipped through his guard faster than the boy he'd grown up with. He made Colton want things he shouldn't even be thinking about.

The guest room upstairs contained no trace of his years living here. Why couldn't he remove all of his feelings for Asher, and leave his heart empty, too?

Asher was still sitting next to him with his legs propped on top of the fat brown coffee table, tapping the toes of his shoes together. He leaned back on one arm and watched the TV, as relaxed as a comfy pillow, only a few inches away from Colton.

"It's Friday night. Don't you have a date? Friends? Something better to do?" Colton groused. "Go away and quit bugging me." He folded his arms tighter. Hopefully it made his biceps bulge, making him look unapproachable.

Asher scooted even closer, sliding across the smooth faux leather of the couch. "Nope. No date."

The whole right side of Colton's body heated and tensed. His ears drank in the beautiful sound of that *no* before he could close them. He pressed his lips together, so they wouldn't tilt up in relief.

"Nothing to do around here except annoy my big brother," Asher said. A gentle dig in his side from Asher's elbow drove the point home. Another waft of spicy cologne scent drifted to his nose.

Colton held his breath and sat up straighter. "I am *not* your brother. I'm not even your stepbrother anymore. The divorce was final like a year ago. I'm just the son of the guy your mom used to be married to. Okay?"

Colder air rushed in between them as the younger man moved away. Colton held his face still, but inside he was wincing. His voice had been too sharp just now, too edgy. If he looked over now, he'd see worry stamped across Asher's usually happy expression.

"Okay. Okay, Cole. It was supposed to be funny. Take a joke."

Colton turned to Asher. Instead of concerned, his face was closed. Whatever he was thinking, it was bolted down behind layers of calm.

He's grown up. Growing away from me. I used to know anything he was thinking. His heart twisted, poking into his chest. Riding on the itchy, annoying prickling, he leaned forward, putting them nose to nose. "I'm just a joke to you."

Asher's face went from cool and remote, to fired-up, in a heartbeat. Colton had to fight back a satisfied smile.

"Don't ever say that," Asher snapped.

They were bare inches apart, closer than Colton had ever let himself get. A skip of panicked excitement scrambled up his spine. He almost leaned back, pulling away, but in the heat of this moment it would be a coward's move. Instead, he lifted his chin and met Asher's angry gaze. Their breath mingled in the charged air between them.

Asher made a little sound, a sort of annoyed huff, and leaned forward. Before he could even begin to interpret that sound, Asher's hand was on the side of his face and their lips were pressed together.

The soft kiss blew straight down through his heart to latch onto his spine, like a lightning strike. From his spine the rush spread out, a wildfire racing through his blood.

I wasn't sure – but he's gay, too! Hot, desperate joy tumbled through him.

When the wildfire reached his stomach, it twisted into a knot and yanked tight. At that moment, Asher was everything. He had held back from thinking about what it would be like for *years* and now, without warning, it was reality.

Asher's fingers trailed at the edge where his hair met skin. Since it made him want to shiver he pressed closer and devoured. With a flick of his tongue he got Asher to open to him. He dove in like a man who has found a pool in the middle of the desert. Exotic spices were in the air, wrapping around him, and his taste was nothing he'd ever let himself imagine.

His traitorous hands were already trailing up the smooth dark fabric covering Asher's back, drawing them tighter together. Nerve endings were sending nothing but bliss to his brain. He leaned into it, couldn't get enough. Without really meaning to, he had pressed Asher over so he was on top and they were both enveloped in the soft puff of the couch. Hardness to hardness, heat to heat, they kissed with an urgent lust which kept him reeling.

It was the way he'd kissed him, out of nowhere. It had knocked Colton off-balance. The unexpected heat must have been why his head was spinning and all of his wires were crossing, making him a sizzling mess. Underneath him Asher wiggled a little, pressing them closer together and knocking Colton's nice, tidy world out of orbit.

A soft moan slipped into his ears. Asher had made that delicious little sound, and hearing it drove the blaze inside Colton to new heights.

The scent of Asher, musky shampoo and *Old Spice* deodorant, was familiar and safe. The shape of his body, on the other hand, all sharp angles and smooth muscles, was new and terrifying. He hadn't known how quick, how strong his response to this would be. He'd been attracted before but not like this. Never with this reckless greed.

This is crazy!

This was Asher. His little brother. *We shouldn't be doing this! Pam could come in, any time, and see me* kissing *her son.*

He yanked his head back, panting, and they both sat back up. It cost him more than he wanted to admit to jerk away, to turn off the blast. Inside, he was still so riled up he could hardly sit still.

In the soft evening light he could see Asher's eyes were darkened by huge, wide pupils. He was smiling. They were still sitting side by side on the couch. So close. Asher was so close. All he had to do was lean forward…

"What—what just happened?" His voice even sounded breathless. *Just make it completely obvious how desperate you are, why don't you?* He cleared his throat and inched back. His ass hit the armrest, and there was nowhere else to go.

Asher's smile disappeared. "That was a kiss, Colton."

"But—no, your mom could come in. I thought you weren't—I mean, you shouldn't—"

Asher shoved away from him and jumped off the couch as if he'd started dripping slime. "I should. I really should have. You have no idea." Throwing up his hands, he spun around and left.

Colton could hear the stomping all the way up the stairs, and his dazed mind floated back to the rare fights Asher had with his mom, years ago. Little kids stomped up the stairs. Eighteen-year-olds on their way to college in two weeks did not.

Part of him wanted to yell up the steps not to tramp like a toddler, but saying anything would be the second stupidest thing he could do right now. The first and most idiotic thing he could do would be to follow him up those stairs and finish their hot kiss. He'd never stop with *just one kiss* if he went up there right now.

Getting up from the couch, he ran a rough hand through his hair and grimaced. The thick strands were an inch or two past the length he usually wanted a haircut.

Asher might like it long. He could get a good grip in it, yank my head back while we—he lowered his hand, as quickly as if his hair had turned red hot.

A walk sounded like the very best idea he'd ever had. He needed some time to shove his feelings about Asher back into the small box he'd put them in, to put the firewall back up that he'd carefully built around them all these years.

Upstairs, Asher's door shut with a soft click. He'd been expecting an echoing *slam*, and he'd been wrong. *Why can't I figure him out anymore?*

He turned around and headed for the front door, the outside air, and some sanity.

Inside his room, Asher threw himself on the bed. With the countdown to his new life at college now measuring in the days, it was a very different room than the one he'd grown up in. Shelves were empty, and the walls were bare. The room already smelled cleaner. His clothes were gone, given away or packed into a suitcase, ready for the dorms.

It was a time for changes, for new adventures.

The urge was strong to march back downstairs and smack Colton's gorgeous, brooding face. Stronger than the wish to hit him, though, was the desire to go on kissing Colton. It was just as amazing as he had always thought it might be. Asher sighed. *Why is he so oblivious?*

Colton had been so stunned, downstairs. So confused. If Asher knew anything about his former stepbrother, it was how methodical he was about everything, how much he liked to have things in a neat row before the next event could happen. Logical. Tidy. Precise. Asher had just smashed through all of his neat little rows like a random, rampaging comet.

It felt so good.

With a sigh, he pressed a hand against his stomach. It hadn't stopped jumping. His lips still tingled. Now that he'd blown that door wide open, he'd never be able to keep himself away from the heat. Smiling, he leaned back into his firm pillow.

Colton might have a problem with the idea. He'd slotted Asher into the *baby brother, take good care* category years and years ago. Once his mind was made up, it was set in stone. Getting him to break out of his old way of thinking would be a challenge. He had a suspicion Colton hadn't really known Asher's sexual preferences, either. He'd been at college for most of Asher's late teen years.

Lucky for him, obstacles only made Asher want to try harder. The only boy he had ever loved was the silly, stupid one who had just slammed the front door on his way outside to sulk.

The only man he would ever love was Colton.

In two weeks he'd be out on his own, testing his wings at the same college Colton attended. By the time their classes started, Colton would be head over heels in love with him. The idea had come to him the instant his mother had mentioned Colton would be spending the week with them. A few hours later it had matured into a full-blown plan, one he had worked hard on.

Step one, finally blast out of the *little brother* box. Step two, seduction. Step three, happily ever after with Colton. He couldn't see any snags.

His feelings had been buried, tied down, throttled away for so long. It was time to let them out, now that there was nothing keeping them apart.

I'm just the son of the guy your mom used to be married to.

Nestling into the pile of pillows, Asher smiled again. Cole was so very right. It was time to let him know how much that changed things.

CHAPTER TWO

"How did you sleep, Colton?"

Colton looked up with his cheeks stuffed full of pancake. She watched as he forced it all down in a big lump and said, "Fine. Thanks, Pam."

Coffee tinted the air from the cup sitting in front of Pamela. She breathed in the scent with gratitude. Her gaze found Colton across the table, while he was busy cutting up more fluffy pancake. His plate, which had been full of pancakes, a cup of orange juice, the butter plate, and his mug were all arranged in front of him. It almost looked like a barricade between him and Asher. What she didn't know was *why* he felt the need for it.

Her son, who could be one possible reason for the barrier, sat across the small wooden table watching Colton over the rim of his own mug. In the morning sunlight pouring in through the kitchen window, his hair had picked up pure streaks of gold. His free hand danced along the edge of the table, tapping and shifting. He'd never been very good at sitting still. Asher got his zest for life, his energy, from her.

Relaxed in her fluffy purple robe, Pam spooned up more raspberries. The closed, calm expression on Asher's face at the moment meant he was thinking over some sort of plan. Going by the way Colton was sucking down coffee with his pancakes, only pausing long enough to scowl at Asher, the plan had something to do with Colton.

Oh, my baby. Did you finally let him know? To cover the jolt of hope, mixed with anxiety, she took another sip out of her

9

own mug. *Not every plan goes the way you think it will, Ash.*

As if he could hear the thought, Asher glanced over at her and gave her a sly little grin. By the time Colton looked up, his face had smoothed back to calm.

Slicing up her pancakes, Pam smiled quizzically at Colton. He'd been frowning while he stared. He rearranged his face into a smile and then hid behind his mug. Pam had already caught the exhausted slump to Colton's shoulders. And a quick retreat behind his mug hadn't hidden the sad attempt at a smile.

He wasn't her stepson anymore, technically, but she'd been the only mother he had for more than ten years, and the fact he wasn't her biological child changed nothing. Whether she was under her selfish ex-husband's thumb, or free, made no difference. She would always want Colton to be safe and happy. The weight he carried around was too heavy for someone who hadn't even hit his twenty-second birthday yet.

It's a sure bet his father isn't helping him carry any of it either, or Colton wouldn't be here with us for his precious vacation week. Her lips tightened as she reached for the syrup in the middle of the table.

Life had heaped more than the usual bad hand on Colton. First, losing his mother to cancer before he was ten, while dealing with a father who handled hard times by shutting them out, along with everyone else the man knew. Then the diagnosis of bipolar disorder and depression in his teens. Chris still wouldn't admit that the two different doctors who had made the same diagnosis were right. Nothing could be wrong with *his* boy, oh no. Not the son who was supposed to be a perfect carbon copy of the father.

Finally, just a little over a year ago, she had become divorced from Chris during Colton's sophomore year of college. *It's about time for something good to happen to him.* Pam cut her pancake into small chunks with vicious, quick movements.

The fastest way to scare Colton off was to smother him with concern, though. When he felt threatened, she had learned, he pulled on an impenetrable coat of armor—a lot like a handsome, brooding turtle with a mile-thick shell.

Casually, Pam pushed over the skillet of scrambled eggs and nudged the salt a little closer to his elbow. "How is school going? All ready for the fall semester?" she asked.

He was staring down at his empty plate as if it was a broken, charred motherboard, waiting to be fixed. "What? Oh, yeah, I'm all ready. I've got another internship set up for September, at a tech firm across town." Reaching for the spoon, he scooped eggs onto his plate and then sat there, just looking at them.

"That's awesome, Cole." For the first time all morning, Asher contributed to the conversation.

Colton's hazel eyes flickered up towards Asher and then fastened back down on his plate. With slow, scowling care Colton forked up a bite of eggs and chewed. He didn't reply. Pam thought she could hear the faint echo of locks snapping shut on thick metal armor.

Asher sat back in his chair, and his chin went up—always a dangerous sign.

"And the job? How are they treating you at the computer store?" Pam said quickly.

Colton stuffed in another bite of eggs and choked it down. "Fine. They were cool about me taking this week off. I thought I'd go to the lake today if it's nice."

He didn't offer to take Asher with him, and Asher didn't ask.

Pam fought to keep the confusion off her face. This morning was out of the ordinary for them. The two had always been close. One of the few things she hadn't worried about when she married Chris was how her son and Chris's son would get along. Seven-year-old Asher had become attached to Colton right from the start, and he had accepted it with more patience than most ten-year-old boys ever had.

Asher was the one person who could sometimes support Colton out of his black periods, just about the only person he would allow close enough to see them.

Giving up all pretenses, Pam asked, "How about your meds? Did you remember to bring the new one with you?"

She didn't need to say. *Please tell me this one is finally working.* She didn't have to say it.

Colton looked her right in the eye when he answered, a clue he wasn't being completely honest. "I brought it. It works great, thanks." He stood up to set his empty plate in the sink.

Asher twirled his fork around between his fingers. The morning light jumped from edge to edge across the dull metal while he sat there without speaking.

Colton didn't look at her again, and she didn't say anything else to him as he left the sun-bright kitchen. The old, familiar worry came trickling back to fill up her throat. Their troubles never stopped worrying her, no matter how big or muscled her babies might look right at the moment.

Pam waited until she couldn't hear Colton's footsteps on the stairs. "Is something wrong with you two? Did you have a fight?" she asked quietly.

With a half-smile, Asher said, "Sort of. Not quite a fight. I need a couple of days to work it out, I think."

Pam nodded, stood up to clear away her own empty plate and moved over to the sink to start filling it with soapy water. "As long as you get it worked out. I'm not sure I believe him about the new meds working great. I don't like how cut-off from everyone he's been since he went to college. We barely see him." She tightened her mouth, to keep away a frown, and dunked her plate in the sudsy sink. "I don't think his friends try hard enough. Colton needs patience and understanding. He's so… alone over there."

"I don't know. Maybe the new one is working. It could just be our fight messing with him right now." Asher got up to add his own plate to the suds and nudged his mother out of the way so he could start loading the dishwasher.

"I'll do a sweep of his room, anyway. Can you keep him out of the house for a while this afternoon?"

Asher's mouth twisted. "If he has any heavy music or depressing movies or whatever, they won't be in his old room here, Mom. They'd be in his apartment. I'll get him out, though. Some vitamin D would be a good thing." He tapped the dirty fork that he was about to add to the dishwasher against his lips, absently. Pam reached out to take it away.

"Maybe I'll beg for a visit to his apartment again. I can double check for sad music there, too. He might think he gets to go to the lake alone, but he's wrong." Grinning, Asher set the last plate inside the dishwasher and opened the cupboard next to it for the soap.

Pam laughed as she turned around to wipe down the kitchen table. Knowing Asher would be helping eased her mind. Stubborn didn't begin to describe her son. He was also fiercely protective and an incurable optimist. She'd chosen an old-fashioned name for him, but it fit her sunny child. "I know that tone. Go easy on him, hon."

Behind his mother's back, Asher's grin turned crafty. Colton didn't know what was about to hit him.

Hard would be a better word for it. Definitely, hard.

Colton gripped the steering wheel and focused on the narrow, winding road to the lake. "Are you sure you didn't have to work today?"

Asher crossed his legs. Colton's eyes tracked over to the

pale sweep of thigh showing under loose red swim shorts and darted away again.

"Friday was my last day. Remember? I'm going to find a job on campus, so I don't have to drive from one end of town to the other in between classes."

Asher shifted a bit closer. Colton leaned away. He was almost squished up against his own driver's side window. The radio muttered along in the background, telling them the weather would be warm and sunny today. Even with the windows down it was boiling in his little truck. His shirt was soaked with sweat, stuck to his back.

"Got any suggestions?" Asher murmured.

"What?"

Just a bit closer and his bare, smooth chest brushed Colton's arm. He shivered.

"Suggestions. Somewhere that's hiring on campus," Asher repeated.

"I don't know any jobs on campus anymore. I've been at Fix It Pixels for two years."

He swallowed when Asher leaned away again, giving him a little space. Not enough, though. The old two-wheel drive pickup had seemed roomy enough when he put down 800 dollars for it, but at the moment it felt like a closet.

"Oh, yeah. I sometimes forget how long it's been. I'll find something. Maybe the cafeteria." Asher shrugged and leaned over to dig around in the bag.

As he hit the blinker and slowed down, getting ready to turn, Colton heard Asher grunt in satisfaction. He sat up with the bright orange bottle of sunscreen in his hand. Colton scanned the road ahead, looking for the entrance to the parking lot with an edge of desperation. *This drive would be easier if Asher's shirt was still on, and if he starts spreading lotion over all those muscles I just might hit a tree.*

"People are jerks when they're hungry. And you'll spend all day cleaning up their messes in the cafeteria," he said, as a distraction. He kept his hands tight on the steering wheel and his eyes glued forward.

"Fine with me. I just need a paycheck, and I spent all day cleaning at the restaurant, anyway. I'm used to it."

Any place would be lucky to hire Asher. He made the day brighter just by smiling. Colton sometimes thought, when he was in a whimsical mood, that Asher's name was the truest thing about him. It meant *joy*.

"You're worth more than cleaning up slop. You can work anywhere you want." His thigh muscle jumped when Asher patted it. He gritted his teeth together.

"I know, and I'll get an amazing job someday. I've got it all planned out. My first semester of college doesn't have to have the coolest job ever. Just a paycheck."

Colton couldn't help the small smile. Asher made plans, all the time, lots of plans. He filled up notebooks with little lists and the word *goals* in big block letters. He color-coded and plastered them with sticky notes. The fact that those plans changed, or didn't happen, hadn't ever discouraged him from going ahead and making more plans. He bounced through life like a goofy little pinball and somehow got where he was going, anyway.

Colton pulled the truck into a parking space, turned off the ignition and was out the door before Asher could say anything else, or make any other moves.

Before he reached the trees, he looked back. Asher was grabbing the big yellow beach bag and their towels from the floorboards, which meant he was bent over and his excellent, tight ass was the easiest part of him to see right now.

If Colton could get to the water, like right now, it wouldn't be so obvious to anyone out here how much he appreciated the sight of Asher in swim shorts. It was ridiculous to have half of a hard-on right now. He turned and started towards the trees again.

"Let's go farther down," Asher said.

Colton turned his head but kept his body faced forward, towards the biggest, busiest beach at the lake.

With a free hand Asher indicated the direction he wanted, off to the right.

Colton narrowed his eyes at the dark mass of pine trees over that direction. There was less chance of people being at the tiny beaches strung out along the east side of the lakeshore. Alarm bells were starting to wake up and clang in his head. He was jumpy enough from riding up alone in the truck with Asher, remembering the sensation of their bodies pressed together every few minutes. Isolated places were only going to make it worse.

No matter how many times he tried, he couldn't force their kiss out of his head. The tangle in his stomach seemed ready to become a permanent resident. It yanked tighter every time Asher moved, and Colton got a whiff of his spicy cologne smell.

Wasn't this why he had buried himself in the college campus for the last three years and didn't come up much for air? To stay away from Asher and the guilty, forbidden feelings the other man stirred up in him? Everything was smoother when Asher wasn't barging in on him watching TV, running around in his hip-hugging sweats, or teasing him and trying to make him laugh.

His mind needled him. *Smoother sure, and lonelier, but dull and dark and missing all the colors.*

He looked at the trees, then back at the man waiting for his answer. Letting Asher come with him to the lake had been a terrible idea, but he couldn't quite deny that part of him *wanted* him there. A tiny piece of Colton, deeply buried and denied, kept whispering to remind him Asher's eighteenth birthday had been more than six months ago.

He'd called to say happy birthday, but he hadn't gone to the party.

Without waiting any longer, Asher started off, winding between the trees. A flicker of red shorts, bright yellow beach bag, gold hair flashing in the sunlight, and then he had slipped between the trees and out of sight.

I could stay right here and swim by myself. He stood at the edge of the asphalt in trunks, shirt, and sandals, holding the truck keys—and nothing else.

Asher took the bag, which means he has both towels. Damnit.

Colton stomped off after him.

CHAPTER THREE

For a while, Asher swam and splashed without going near Colton. The sun was high enough to spread dazzling sparkles across the lake when he finally left the water for his towel.

A breeze ruffled the surface of the lake into gentle waves and dried him off while he dozed in the shade under the trees. A sharp pine smell dominated the air, but he could also smell the murky green of the plants flourishing by the water and the earth baking in the summer sunlight. A few flies buzzed past but didn't stop to pester him.

He hadn't bothered to look when Colton disappeared off to the side and out of sight, swimming with long, smooth strokes. Cole was like a cat, in some ways. He needed his space, and his space plus some extra when you were making him feel uncomfortable. Pushing him, herding him, was a great way to make him run far and fast.

Tilting his face up to the dappled, tree-shade sunlight, Asher let the grin spread. *Isn't it lucky for the stubborn, silly guy I know him so well?* None of Colton's partners had shown the patience needed to catch him. Asher couldn't recall a boyfriend who had lasted past a year. They didn't want to spend the time to break through those high guards Colton had put up.

Cold silence from Colton's father just added to the complications. Although he wasn't actively bigoted about it, Chris had never really accepted his son was gay. He had a quiet, icy and very *definite* way of making any boyfriends feel unwanted when Colton had the courage to bring them around.

Colton should stand up to his dad, get in his face loud and clear, and tell him to back off. Asher was firm in his opinion. If a toxic person was in your life, the healthiest thing you could do was to cut them out of it. Colton had come close, a few times, to laying down the law, but his father had a sneaky, nasty way of dealing with those attempts. Whenever Chris heard something he didn't want to, he just mentally erased it. *Poof!* No longer part of his memories. He would act like you were crazy if you brought it up.

Asher had an edge there over Colton's exes, because he was already partly inside those defensive walls, and what Chris thought or tried to block out couldn't bother him less.

If Colton was his lover, Chris would *never* have the chance to hurt him again.

There was nothing he didn't know about Colton — and love. His serious, strong face with its dreamy hazel eyes was only the beginning. That lean, gorgeous body Asher had been admiring for so many years was only the wrapping of the package. Most people never got past the face and if they did, they ran head-on into the aloof manner and his guarded conversations.

Cole didn't really know how intimidating he looked when he was uncomfortable. His reaction there was what his father had taught him — shut down, turn away, and ignore it until it went away. In social situations it tended to make strangers angry or uncomfortable as well.

The secret was, inside his cold exterior surged a wide river of deep warmth. It would have surprised both of his former lovers to hear about it. Hidden from the world, Colton contained enough strength to shrug off a critical, self-centered father and hold up the burden of his depression at the same time. Loyal, sad, affectionate, silly, intelligent, wounded, bone-headed, and tough, all of those things de-scribed Colton. No obstacles were holding Asher back from showing him how much he loved all of those many pieces.

Starting now.

Splashing from the direction of the water warned Asher. Colton was getting out. He turned on his side to indulge in the spectacular view of a long, lithe body emerging from the lake, dripping wet. His hands itched to follow the path of those shining drops of water clinging to Colton's muscled abs as they slid toward the top of his shorts.

Familiar and achy, warm coils of lust knotted low in his stomach at the sight. Finally, *finally*, he was going to let that knot unwind and see what happened when it did.

Cold water splashed on his legs, interrupting his ogling. He yelped.

"Jerk! I'm drying off." He laughed.

While he pouted his lips to mock-glare, Colton wore a ra-re grin.

Colton grabbed the water bottle out of the bag lying next to the towels and took a healthy swig. "You'll still dry—it's hot today. Man, I've missed coming here." He plopped down onto his own towel and swigged some more water.

"M-hmm," Asher agreed. He was starving for another taste of those gorgeous full lips. "Hey, Colton?"

"What?"

"Put some more sunscreen on my back?"

With the water bottle still raised, Colton froze.

Asher nudged the little bottle over to the side of his towel. "It's been a couple of hours and I need to put more on." He rolled over onto his stomach and waited, breathless with anticipation.

Asher's heartbeat thudded in his ears, once, twice, three times, before he saw Colton's feet moving out of the corner of his eye. He turned his head down into the towel to hide the smile he knew had to be full of victory. It would make

Colton suspicious, and he would be right.

Asher sensed the warmth without looking when Colton sat next to him on the smooth rocks of their tiny cove. He held still, body singing with the expectancy of Colton's touch. In front of them, the lake was deserted. Nothing but the wind moved on either side of them. There was no time like now.

In another few heartbeats Asher felt a hand moving across his back, leaving a cool trail of sunscreen behind. Using both hands, Colton smoothed the lotion up and down.

Behind the coolness from the lotion came waves of fierce heat, pulsing through Asher. Everything from his nipples down to the front of his bathing suit went tight. He wanted those lips on his again, his tongue inside Colton's mouth. He wanted to dive back into the warmth with both feet, heart pounding.

Turning over, he sighed, stretched. "Thanks. Can't be too careful with this stupid pale skin." Cole's eyes were right where he wanted them, on the obvious evidence of how aroused he was. The other man sat with his knees pulled up, probably hiding some evidence of his own.

"It's not—" Colton's voice was husky, and he cleared his throat. "It's not stupid pale skin. It's like a pearl."

Asher couldn't help laughing a little, even as he throbbed. Colton had yet to move his eyes higher than the crotch of his bathing suit. "That's so nice of you and so untrue. It's ghostly." He sat up and reached across to grab the sunscreen out of Colton's hand with slow, smooth movements, letting skin slide against skin.

"Now yours"—he motioned for Colton to turn around and he did, looking dazed—"yours is this perfect olive tan color. The sun only makes it look better. I wish mine would tan like that."

He took his time, feeling each separate swell of muscle on

the wide shoulders before he spread more sunscreen down Colton's long back in deliberate, wide circles. In the quiet around the lake he could hear Colton's breath shorten, catch, and release in a ragged exhale.

Going with his instincts, he leaned forward to press a soft kiss just under his ear and then started to nibble gently on his earlobe.

Colton jerked. "What are you doing?"

"Kissing you," he said and pressed another kiss to the curve of his neck. He smelled like sunshine and water, sunscreen and male, all at the same time.

"Not a good idea." Desperation edged his tone.

"Tell me to stop, then," Asher challenged. Smoothly, he moved around so they were face to face. Colton stayed frozen, sitting on the damp towel and staring at him. In the center of the hazel, his pupils were huge, dark and dilated.

Asher leaned forward to press soft kisses to his cheek, the stubble dusting his firm jaw, the luscious mouth he had been aching to taste all day. His hands were busy stroking the line of Colton's bare shoulders, rubbing down his biceps.

Wind picked up across the lake, pushing up waves to lap at the rocky shore in front of them. Up in the trees a blue jay called, harsh and loud. Neither of them noticed.

"Asher," Colton murmured. There was a warning in his tone, a hint of barrier Asher ignored to focus on the beautiful sound of his name rumbling out in Cole's deep voice.

"Don't worry so much about everything," he begged. "Sometimes you need to let things happen."

Asher pressed a soft kiss to the pulse beating fast in Colton's neck, nipping at the side of his neck gently. He gave himself the immense pleasure of letting his hands run over the smooth, bare line of Colton's back.

Colton swore and ended the curse with a kiss. When his control broke, it went like a dam and released floods of heat.

His mouth was everywhere, as hot and impatient as Asher's, while his hands came up to stroke through his hair. Asher filled himself with the sensation of Colton touching him, dove into it, and drowned in it.

Bending forward, he pressed tiny kisses to his chest. He felt Colton gasp when he circled a nipple with his tongue. He'd had years to learn his mind, and now he wanted to learn his body. Every dip, every muscle.

Impatient and needy, he pressed the other man backward onto the towel and continued stroking, exploring. When he kissed his way down from his chest to a taut, flat stomach, Cole jolted under his mouth. The jump of muscles under his lips aroused him as much as the harsh breathing shivering out into the quiet air.

On a groan, Colton grabbed his arms and yanked him back up for a deep, hard kiss. Asher couldn't think, could barely breathe. Kissing him was everything he'd ever imagined and more.

Colton shifted and rolled them over so he was on top and they were pressed together, heat to heat. Swimsuits were no barrier—he could feel every inch of Colton's slim body and exactly how much Colton loved this. Giving in to the need pounding through him, he arched upwards, letting his hips rise to meet the hardness pressed against him, and groaned.

"Shit, Asher," Colton breathed out. He kissed his way down Asher's jaw to his throat, leaving a blazing trail of fireworks.

When Colton reached his chest he kept going, pressing damp kisses in widening circles. It took the smallest shift in angle for him to sweep his tongue over a nipple, and the sharp thrill of it made Asher shudder. While his mouth stayed busy with darting, hot kisses, he trailed his hand down to caress Asher's thigh. So close. So close to where he ached for Colton's touch.

Afraid, amazed, and aroused to a razor-sharp pitch, he heard his own breathing become as ragged as Cole's.

He reached his wandering hand over to stroke Colton through his swim shorts. In return, Cole leaned down to catch Asher's earlobe in a gentle bite. He couldn't keep his own hands from wandering down the smooth chest to the trail of curly hair leading down into Colton's own shorts. He was damp and hot, already slippery, and Asher couldn't wait to explore.

"Colton." He sighed. "Do you know how wonderful you are?"

A long, deep sigh shuddered out of the man on top of him. Colton eased back, nudging Asher's hand away, and let his head sink down to rest on his chest. "I don't know why you'd think so, especially right now. Jesus, Ash, I shouldn't be groping you like this."

Asher squeezed his eyes shut and wrapped his arms around him. They were pressed together like lovers, the way he had hoped, but it was clear Colton was going to need some more time to see it the same way. Asher's heart was still pounding at the touch of all that bare, warm skin. He wasn't sure how much time he'd be able to give.

"Quit. Quit thinking about *shouldn't*. I started it, anyway. I wouldn't have kissed you unless I wanted you to kiss me, okay? Stop feeling all guilty and — and brotherly," he demanded.

When Colton started to shift away, he held him closer. Instead of running to the other end of the forest the way he probably wanted to, Colton ended up stretched on top of Asher, full length, with his head buried in the curve of Asher's neck.

He went ahead and snuck a quick kiss to the dark hair, while he was there anyway. He still yearned for the touch of those strong hands, but he told himself to quit for now.

Things were moving too fast for Colton, and he needed to catch up.

Against his neck Colton's lips moved as he gave a soft laugh. "*Brotherly* is not on the list of feelings I'm feeling right now."

Colton heaved over and rolled onto the bare ground next to Asher. In a gesture that spoke of frustration, both of his hands came up to cover his face and scrub. "What is going on, Asher? Why are we doing this? I can't think straight around you anymore."

"We're doing this because it's time to. I've *wanted* to kiss the hell out of you for years. God, Cole, you're so oblivious sometimes."

"Yeah, right," he said and laughed.

Asher sat up, grabbed his hands, and yanked them apart so he could look him in the eye. "Cole. I'm being serious. I've" — *loved you* — "had a crush on you for a long time. But it was awkward with our parents being married. Then you were eighteen, and I wasn't and it just never seemed like a good time. Now it is."

Colton stared at him. His face was stunned and almost guilty. Asher wondered if he'd had some of the same thoughts, all those years. A little thrill skipped up his spine, at the thought.

"You said it yourself," he reminded him. "You're just the son of the guy my mom *used* to be married to, now." He let go of Colton's wrists.

"I — yeah, I *said* that but I didn't mean for this" — Colton waved a hand, indicating the two of them, alone, barely clothed — "to start. We can't just — it's not — "

Moving with slow deliberation, Asher leaned forward, giving Colton time to hold him back or move away. He did neither.

The tension between them instantly flew back up to danger level. "We can do this, and it is happening. This is your fair warning, Colton." He leaned closer to press a kiss to the corner of his mouth. "I'm changing how it is between us." He kissed the other corner. "I'm going to give it my best try." The next kiss was light, teasing, full on the lips.

A shaky sigh escaped Colton, and Asher smiled.

"Oh," Colton said.

CHAPTER FOUR

Tuesday morning Colton was up just after the sun, rested and ready to go. After a quick breakfast of oatmeal and blueberries he rinsed his bowl and tossed it in the dishwasher.

With barely hidden glee he walked over to stand right in front of Asher, who was sitting at the table finishing the last sips from his mug. "Hey, let's go."

"What?" Asher peered up at him, blinking. Colton pretended the mess of bright, morning-tousled hair wasn't ridiculously attractive. "Go where?" Colton saw a suspicious expression spread wide over his face as Asher took another sip of what Colton and Pam liked to call his *milk and sugar with a little bit of coffee.*

"For a jog. Regular exercise is good for me," Colton said. He clamped down on his smile when Asher's eyes narrowed even further. He suspected something, oh yes he did. "I like jogging. I thought you'd like to go, too."

Putting the mug down on the table, Asher buried his face in his hands and scrubbed. "I hate running."

Colton didn't try to hide the sardonic lift to his eyebrow. "It gives you lots of endorphins and stuff. It's really good for you."

The glare Asher shot up at him was killer. He met it with another sunny smile and a careless tilt of his head. "It lifts your mood. It will lift *my* mood. You know, make sure my medication has the best chance to work." Asher shrugged and reached for his coffee again. Colton waited a beat, for dramatic effect, and then played his ace. "I'd like to spend some time with you."

Asher's hands tightened around his mug, and his eyes went from narrowed to wide. His frown softened. Then he sighed. "Fuck. Fine. Give me a couple of minutes to change into sweats or something."

Nodding, still smiling, Colton sat down to drink some water and wait.

He had noticed that Pam had been eyeing both of them from across the table. When he looked over at her she smiled and lifted an eyebrow. There was something sly in her smile. Immediately, he dialed his own smirk down from *satisfied* to *plain happy*.

He didn't want Pam guessing something was going on when nothing was. Nothing. He just wanted Asher to see how much work was involved living with bipolar disorder. How much constant vigilance he needed for everything he ate, all of the activities he chose, even the movies he watched. Asher would get tired of it, in a week or less, and give up on this crazy idea about them being together.

So Pam doesn't need to know a thing.

There was nothing for her to know, in the first place. Those steamy kisses were all in the past. All forgotten. No matter how much his hormones and his heart urged him towards Asher.

He deserved better than Colton. He deserved the best.

"I think I'll go into the office today," Pam said. She was sipping her own black tea, a touch of cunning still sneaking into her smile.

"I thought you had the week off, for Asher's last few days at home?" Colton asked.

"Mmm, I do, but there was a mini-crisis with a contract going through escrow yesterday. I think I should go in and help handle it. Just for a few hours. I'll be back before lunch. Tell Asher for me, will you?"

Colton nodded, although he wanted to beg her to stay. Pam being in the same house was an extra layer of security, keeping his actions pure. Could he stay away from Asher, stick to the plan, if he knew they were alone?

In the sunny kitchen, he straightened his shoulders and stiffened his spine. Of course he could. It was best for Asher if he could move on to college free and clear. He would always be able to do what was best for Asher.

"All right then. Thanks, Colton. I'll text so you know when I'm heading home. You two have a good day while I'm gone. Go do something fun, after your jog." With a wave, Pam headed out of the kitchen door. He heard her keys jangle as she found them in the front hall.

The door clicked open, then shut, and her footsteps crunched down the driveway. A few seconds later her sensible *BMW* purred to life. Then she was backing down the drive. Going, going, gone.

Asher slouched into the kitchen in light gray sweatpants, a tight blue shirt, and tennis shoes. His glorious blond hair was brushed and swept back, framing his grumpy face.

Looking at him, drenched in bright sunshine, Colton's mouth went dry. *Maybe I could call Pam and make up an emergency.*

"Are we going or what?" Asher asked. "Let's get this over with."

Right. He was deploying exercise to annoy Asher out of his life. Colton stood up and gestured to the door. "After you."

An hour later Asher struggled up the driveway behind Colton, cursing him silently. His calves burned, his thighs were unhappy, and he was covered in sweat. He was going to get Colton for this morning of running. The poor man had no idea what revenge lay in store.

Ahead at the end of the driveway, Colton was already unlocking the front door. The only good part of the run had been watching him jog along in front, enjoying the way his ass looked in those comfy dark shorts. The dark vee of sweat trailing down his shirt was a nice bonus, as well. Asher could imagine his tongue following that same trail downward. Colton would taste salty, and his skin would feel hot. The idea had kept Asher going for the last half-mile.

"Next time." He panted as he came up the steps behind Colton. "I pick — the exercise." He sucked in air, let it out in a whoosh. "And I'm picking something better, like bike riding. I can ride a bike a lot farther than I can run."

Colton shrugged and led the way inside.

Asher dashed up the stairs, although it killed his thighs a bit more. He'd zip down the hallway and into the upstairs bathroom before Colton could, forcing him to make a choice. There was another shower downstairs... or he could join Asher in the upstairs bathroom, if the idea occurred to him and if he wanted to.

Glancing back, he caught Colton watching as he got up to the top stair. The other man's eyes were definitely focused on how well Asher's sweatpants fit him. The idea was going to occur to him.

Biting back a grin, he hurried down the hallway.

His mom was at the office, and bless her for going. Asher was going to get clean and stay naked. Then he was going to find Colton, no matter which shower he ended up using, and lick every inch of the body he had been admiring from behind. If Colton thought making him go out for a jog was going to irritate him out of his plan, he was sadly mistaken.

He hurried into the bright, white, tiled bathroom, stripping off his sweaty clothes as he went. The door stayed unlocked and propped open behind him. *This seduction would go a lot faster if Colton would just join me in the shower.*

Just in case, he stuck his head out of the door. Colton was standing, frozen, in front of his bedroom door, just a few feet away. Asher let the door swing open a few more inches—well aware he was standing there stark naked—and watched Colton's eyes zero in on his dick. It twitched at the attention.

"I'm going to take a quick shower," Asher said. *Like it isn't obvious.* "You want to join me?"

Colton swallowed. "What?" He sounded vague and dazed.

"Do you want to take a shower with me?" Asher repeated.

"Wha—no. No, I'm good," Colton said, scowling. He turned around and yanked his bedroom door open.

Asher rolled his eyes and turned around to get in the shower. It was going to have to be quick. His whole body ached for Colton to be pressed up against it.

Soaping up, scrubbing his hair, and rinsing took a little less than ten minutes. Scraping the towel over him took another minute. Asher dropped the wet towel in a heap on the floor, which would have gotten him a *look* from Pam, and went in search of some sexy time.

When Asher got downstairs and opened the bathroom door, he saw that Colton was just stepping out of his own shower. Asher watched as Colton seemed to freeze, standing there, dripping on the plush blue rug, with one hand stretched out to grab a towel.

The lock *clicked* behind Asher as he got a good, long look at all the lean muscles on display, and the way Colton was coming to attention as he looked at Asher. Balmy, sweet, liquid lust blew through him. He knew his cheeks were flushed. He was already hard and throbbing.

"Asher," Colton said warningly. "You shouldn't be in here like this."

"Okay."

Colton backed up a step and then another. When he hit the edge of the tub he had nowhere else to go. "Seriously." He chuckled, nerves ringing through the laugh. "Your — your mom could be back any second."

"Okay. We'd better hurry, then." The idea gave him an extra, deviant little thrill. He took the step needed to press their bodies together. Colton was still backed into the edge of the spotless white bathtub.

Warm, moist air from the shower wrapped around him as he gripped Colton's hip with one hand. The steam wrapping around them smelled like Colton's usual choice of bar soap, and it made Asher smile. With his other hand he held the back of Colton's neck, using it to pull him forward for a kiss. He kissed him like he'd wanted to all day, devouring until he was lightheaded.

Colton's hands had come up to wrap around him. He stroked up and down Asher's back, dipping down to caress his ass. Asher's cock jerked in response, so he dug his hands into Colton's long, dark hair and pulled him even closer.

"Ash." Colton's voice was hoarse. "You shouldn't be in here, doing this. You need someone better for you." In direct contradiction to his words, his fingers gripped Asher tightly, pulling them tight together.

Asher sighed and nipped at his collarbone, then licked the spot he had bit. "Why don't you leave it up to me?" He reached down and closed a hand around Colton, finding him all thick and warm and ready.

Colton's eyes fluttered closed, and he groaned. "God... you're going to regret this someday. All those... smart, normal guys in your... classes. One of them has to be gay, too." He panted harshly, and his fingers dug into Asher's back hard enough to bruise.

Asher started stroking a little harder, to shut him up. "That's my problem. My choice." He played his thumb around the tip of Colton's shaft, collecting and spreading the pre-cum. "Don't give a shit about any hypothetical guys in my classes. And I don't think I'll ever regret this." He leaned forward to start kissing Colton again, slipping his tongue in between his wide-open lips. His hips thrust forward, yearning towards friction.

He sighed in relief when Colton's hand drifted down to grip him in return. It was hard to keep up a rhythm and kiss at the same time. They were sloppy, their teeth knocked together once, he couldn't breathe, and he didn't care. The pleasure of having Colton's hands around him was so sharp it stung, prickling along every nerve ending.

Tension was building to impossible heights, winding tighter and tighter, deep down inside him. Groaning, he broke their kiss and threw his head back to gasp in some air. Colton nipped at the exposed arch of his throat, making him jump. So close—he was *so* close.

He could tell Colton was, too, throbbing in his hand, hot as a summer afternoon. Increasing his speed a little more, Asher felt Colton's hand moving faster in mirrored tempo. He had to grip the hard plastic edge of the bathroom sink next to him as his hips bucked.

Legs trembling, he sucked in damp shower air and let the ecstasy come—and heard the hard, echoing rap of a knock on the bathroom door.

Colton froze into dead stillness in front of him. Asher had to force down a moan of disappointment.

"Asher? Are you in there?"

He let go of the sink to clutch Colton tight around the hip with one hand and kept stroking with the other. Colton looked terrified, but he didn't pull away. "I'm here, Mom."

"Are you taking a shower? And where's Colton?"

Asher licked up the taut column of Colton's neck. Still working him with smooth pulls, he reached around to toy at the crease of Cole's very fine ass with a finger.

Colton sucked in a gasp and then tried to hide the noise, burying his face in Asher's hair. Asher was as hard as he'd ever been — knowing how close they were to being caught. He'd never had any idea he was so perverted.

"Just finished," he grated out. "Don't know where Colton is. Somewhere." Above him, he felt Colton's muffled laugh.

Finally, Colton's hand came back to wrap around Asher's cock again, and his hips shot forward in response. He could have melted into Colton's firm grip, fallen down in a gooey puddle of lust right here on the linoleum. In two days he had already started to need Colton's touch. It would be even easier to start craving the way his heart was knocking painfully against his ribs, love and panic merging into one hot mess as he felt Colton let go of his control a little.

"Okay, well, if he's not in the upstairs bathroom, I need to use it."

"Sure," Asher breathed out. Colton tweaked one of his nipples, rolling it between two fingers, and he choked on air.

"Are you all right, hon? You sound strange," Pam said from the other side of the door.

"Fine," he gasped. "Stupid... jog maybe. I'm not doing that again. Be out... in a minute."

"Okay." She didn't sound convinced, but he heard the sweet, sweet sound of her footsteps moving away.

When he couldn't hear her steps anymore, he took his cue to dive back into pleasuring Colton. He found a rhythm that let him squeeze the top of Colton's cock, collecting the moisture pooling there to make his strokes smoother. Every pull was answered with a slightly different gasp, a stifled moan. They filled Asher's ears like music. He kissed Colton hard, nipping at his lower lip.

At the same time, Colton had his own frantic pace on Asher's shaft. Too much — the feeling was almost too much.

He was going to come soon. He'd die if he didn't.

Muscles shaking, he let the pleasure build and build. When he felt Colton spasm under his hand, when he heard the long, low groan, he let himself go. The world fell away into nothing but stars, and he was deaf and blind to anything but the pleasure filling him up and hollowing him out.

"God," Colton said. Asher opened his eyes. Colton was staring at him, looking stunned. "What are we *doing*? Your mom —"

Asher's legs felt weak and watery, so he let himself slide down to sit with his back against the wall. The mist in the air chilled his overheated body, and he shivered, relaxing into the aftershocks. "Didn't come in. We're not going to scar her for life."

Colton stayed standing, shifting sideways to lean against the wooden vanity cabinet instead of the tub. "Asher —"

"Don't even think about saying it." Asher raised his hand in a *stop* gesture. He couldn't stand to hear about how this was a bad idea when his body was still tingling from Colton's touch. He closed his eyes and drew in a deep breath. "This was not a mistake. I'm not going to change my mind."

When he felt Colton's hand start to rub his shoulder, soothingly, he looked up.

"I was actually going to ask if you want to be the first one to try to sneak upstairs. We'd better be quick."

"Oh." Asher tilted his head to stare at Colton, double-checking his expression for sincerity. "Yeah. You'd probably better go first. She already knows I'm in here."

He heaved himself off the floor to reach for the washcloth they would both need, from the little shelf above the toilet.

Colton caught him by surprise, reaching out to cup the back of his neck and draw him in for a good, hard kiss. Instantly, he was lost. His mother and her entire book club could have barged in, and he wouldn't care if he could just keep kissing Cole. When they finally broke apart, he had to remind himself why there was a washcloth dangling from his hand.

He was still wiping up when Colton leaned in front of him to swipe the towel off of the rack. He smiled at him, softly.

Cole had the door unlocked and had started through it before he could take a step. The mischief in his answering smile hooked Asher's heart, hard.

"Hey, Ash?" Colton asked.

"Hmm?" He was dizzy with love, watching Colton grin.

"You know, there's only one towel down here."

"What?"

The door was already clicking closed. Asher bent over to yank open the vanity cabinet and let out a short curse. Colton was right. He'd just taken the only towel.

Laughing helplessly, Asher shook his head and prepared for his washcloth-covered run of shame down the hallway, up the staircase, and all the way to his room.

Chapter Five

When Colton didn't come downstairs for breakfast on Wednesday morning, Asher wasn't surprised. Going into a full retreat was so very like him after a big change had rocked his sturdy foundation. He always needed some time to adjust to the new balance, and Asher wasn't really giving him much.

He stayed busy during the morning, going over his fall semester schedule with his mother. They looked over the email assigning a roommate, which had finally come last week. They amused themselves for almost an hour finding the future dorm mate online and decided the two would probably get along fine. That was a pretty safe bet, no matter who the roommate was. Getting Asher to dislike someone took lots of sincere, malicious action on that person's part.

Close to lunchtime the phone rang.

On the caller ID, Asher saw it was one of the few people in the world who had put in good, hard effort to make him hate them. Iced tea in one hand and the phone in the other, he answered.

"Hello, Chris." The lack of warmth in his tone was customary, and as usual would go unnoticed by his ex-stepfather.

"Asher. Is your mother there?"

Looking right at Pam, Asher said, "Nope. Grocery shopping. Can I help you?"

A heavy sigh over the phone. "Is my son there?"

Not *your stepbrother* or *Colton*, he noticed. "He is. Can I take a message for you?"

"Is he out right now? I need to speak to him about this semester's tuition."

Having plenty of disposable income didn't make someone an open, generous person. Chris paid for Colton's education, it was true. He provided for him. *Is it too much to ask for him to also spend some of his time, maybe even some emotion on his only child? Obviously it is. Chris is the most selfish person I know.* Asher's fingers tightened around his glass, following the familiar train of thought.

"No, he's still in his room. Let me go see if he's ready to get up," he said, on his way up the stairs.

He cracked open the door, registered the blanket-covered bump still on the bed in the dark room and shut it again, all in one quick move.

"Sorry, he's still sleeping. Let me get a pen or something to write your message down."

"It is not acceptable for him to still be sleeping at this time of day." Somehow the man's tone didn't freeze the tea in Asher's hand over the phone.

Has Colton been taking his meds this week? Asher couldn't watch every move he made. It was very possible he hadn't been, though. "Isn't it? It is one of the known side effects of bipolar disorder, exhaustion. Sort of the way poor appetite is. He hasn't eaten yet today, either." He pictured Chris's wince at the dreaded word, bipolar, and grinned.

Another heavy sigh. "We've discussed this before, many times. It's all in his mind. He just needs to get up, get out of bed, and get over it. If he'd just try *harder* I'm sure he —"

"We *have* been over this, Chris, many times. It's surprising you don't get it yet. Bipolar disorder and depression are related to physical differences in the brain. It is not *all in his mind.* They are just as valid a disease as having a faulty heart valve, or bad vision." His fingers splintered into the phone. *Why can't he just understand? We've been over this again and again*. Fast and frenzied, his heartbeat drummed into his ears. *God, what an asshole.*

"I realize this might not fit in with your and Pam's wishy-washy view of the world, but please go in there and wake him up. I need to speak to him about his classes. Giving in to his little episodes will only make them worse."

"I thought it was about his *tu-i-tion*," Asher enunciated, "and I'm sure you can just have me write a message down for him. When he wakes up we will take all the reasonable steps we can to lift the levels of serotonin in his brain. We'll get him some breakfast. *Then* I will give him your message." He rolled his eyes.

"Serotonin? What is this new nonsense? You're throwing around words a doctor should be using, and you're not even in college yet."

Hearing the sneer in his voice, Asher had no trouble picturing Chris's handsome, frozen face. Like his son, Chris had the fine bone structure, the full lips, the dark, sweeping hair and fierce eyebrows.

Unlike his son, he had no grip on the reality of bipolar disorder.

"It's lucky I'm going to college to *become* a doctor then, isn't it?" he asked, sweet as a sugared scorpion. "I'll learn even bigger words, and I'll use them, too. And someday when I'm helping find the root cause of bipolar disorder I'll be so happy to take my findings, write them up in a nice long report, and then roll my report up, take it, and shove it up your cold—"

The phone was lifted out of his hands, sliding past his ear, before he could complete his satisfying vision of the future. He turned around to see Colton, in athletic shorts and a frayed t-shirt with scruffy bed-hair sticking up, all brown angles and tufts. He grinned crookedly, and Asher's heart stuttered.

"Hey, Dad. I'm up. What's going on?" Colton said into the phone. His eyes went from sleepy to angry as Asher watched, and his brows snapped together. "That's not okay to say. Don't ever say that about him again. In fact, don't call and talk to Asher. I have a cell phone."

Asher edged away and started back down the stairs to let his mother know Colton was awake.

Several minutes later Colton came downstairs to put the phone back in its kitchen cradle, then slumped into the nearest chair. He'd smoothed his hair down, but he still needed a shave. Underneath his closed eyes, the shadows were a deep purple. He wouldn't look all the way up at Asher when he said *good morning*. The only reply he made was a grunt.

A sigh slipped out of Asher, but he kept it quiet so Colton wouldn't hear it and be hurt. Pretending yesterday never happened was apparently the coping mechanism of choice for this morning. He'd let it stand until Colton looked less exhausted and then destroy it.

"Is everything set for your semester, Cole?" Pam asked, from over by the sink. She continued to spread mayonnaise on whole grain bread while Asher finished slicing leftover ham, wielding the kitchen knife with rough enthusiasm. Talking to Chris always had that effect on him.

"Yeah," Colton said. His head was tucked nearly between his shoulders, slumped in defeat, while he leaned over to grab a glass of water.

Pam and Asher traded looks.

After gulping down the whole glass at once, Colton went to the sink and re-filled it. Staring at the bubbling trickle of water into his glass, he admitted, "Not really. Dad's having some finance — issues right now. He said he couldn't pay anything for this semester. He said I should think about taking a break, maybe working at his company for a while, until he can get things turned around."

Without replying, Pam set a plate of sandwiches on the table, added a bowl of baby carrots and the yogurt ranch dip she loved to make. Asher set plates on the table and got out cranberry juice for his own drink.

They had all started eating before Pam finally said, "The divorce is still losing him clients, I suppose." To her credit, her voice was entirely free of the satisfaction it could have held. They all knew that Chris only attended his ultra-conservative Megachurch to maintain good relationships with the rich families he managed finances for. Asher, personally, doubted that Chris had ever had a sincere thought about God in his life. He was nothing but ecstatic that Chris's clients were pissed about him committing the biblical sin of divorce.

"I had an unusually good year, myself," she continued. "A big home over in the Northwest part of town and a duplex downtown and... " Asher watched her survey how tight Colton was holding himself, how tired he looked, and trail off. Her smile mixed equal parts worry and sympathy. "Can you show me your class list? Maybe we could work something out."

From across the table Colton's eyes met hers. "No, I can't let you do that, Pam. I've been applying for scholarships this summer. I got one out of the bunch I applied for, it will cover two thousand dollars of this semester. I can just — drop the classes I can't afford or something."

"It's your *last year*," Pam reminded him. "Just these last two semesters. Your last year is worth paying for." Watching him open his mouth to argue, she cut in quickly. "If it makes you so uncomfortable to take the help, think of it as a loan. You can pay me back. We'll write up a payment schedule and everything."

He closed his mouth. It seemed like he would at least consider the offer.

Asher noticed Colton had only gotten through half of his sandwich. Exhaustion and no appetite. It looked like Colton was definitely headed for a down day today.

Colton caught Asher's scrutiny and lifted an eyebrow at him. "So you're going to be, what, like a neurosurgeon?" he asked. A tiny edge of surprise was clear in his voice.

"Well, not a surgeon." Asher snagged a carrot and twirled it in the dip on his plate. "I feel like throwing up when I think about cutting into people. I want to get into research. I've been looking it up. I need some sort of medical degree, with a lot of emphasis on biology. A graduate degree in neurology would help."

Both eyebrows were up now. "That's—I did not know you wanted to be a doctor—impressive."

He smiled. "Let's get me through this first semester, to start with. Oh, we found out who my roommate is today."

They filled the rest of the meal with chatter about the upcoming semester. Pam didn't bring up a loan for tuition again. Colton only ate about three-quarters of his sandwich, and none of the vegetables.

While they cleaned up the table Asher handed him the bowl of carrots to put away. He stepped close, right into his space, daring Colton to step back. Colton stayed put, but he flashed a quick, guilty glance at Pam.

Pam was gathering the plates off of the table and only smiled.

Asher made sure to keep his eyes wide and innocent when he looked at Colton. "Can I see your new med? If I'm going to be a doctor I need to know about these things. And you can give me your perspective on how well it works, too."

Asher was aware that Colton knew when they were trying to get him to take his meds, even when it was sort of subtle. Colton's smile was very dry as he turned away to set the carrots in the fridge. "Sure. We're trying Lamictal now," Colton told him. Asher led the way out of the kitchen as Colton followed.

"And it's an antidepressant?" Asher asked, genuinely curious.

"An anticonvulsant, if you want to be technical." They were halfway up the stairs. Trudging along behind him, Asher could tell Colton was moving with less than his usual energy.

Inside his room Colton went to his black duffel bag to rummage around while Asher went to throw open the heavy brown curtains and let some sun in. It used to drive Colton crazy when he would do that on school mornings. Even without the depression Colton was not much of a morning person.

From the bright frame of the window he turned around and took the little white bottle Colton held out. "Lamotrigine," he read out. "It's a new one, isn't it? They had you trying Lithium last time if I remember right. What, three years ago?"

"Three years," Colton agreed tiredly. Colton wandered past him, over to the window to tug the curtains down again, back to the bed to zip up the duffel. Colton's movements were robotic. Like he didn't even have to think about wanting the window closed and the light gone.

Asher shrugged and walked over to the doorway to peer at the bottle in the light from the hallway. After he scanned the dosage information on the back of the little bottle he snapped off the top to shake out one of the tiny pills.

He held it out to Colton, pulling his mouth up into a smile. It was supposed to be encouraging, without being too pushy.

Colton didn't take it.

In two short steps he was close enough to look Colton in

43

the eye. One more step and he was nearly pressed against Cole's broad chest. Invisible inside his fist, the medicine was a little round spot of hardness.

Colton's breath brushed warm against his lips, and it made him ache. Every nerve ending leaped to life, urging him towards the man standing like a mute wall in front of him. "Take the pill, Colton." He brushed a light kiss across those closed lips. Colton didn't kiss him back, this time.

"Asher... " Air rushed between them when Colton stepped away. He retreated to the far side of his bed, deep in shadow, and stood there. "We have to stop doing this. I'm not who you should be with. You're going to college in a few days. There will be plenty of guys in your med program." Blurry, pale movements in the dark showed him Colton was crossing his arms in front of his chest. "You should try for one of them. I'm too messed up. Just—find someone better. Someone normal. I screw up everything I touch."

From his little pool of light in the doorway Asher could see Colton's head lower, defeated. His fingers were clenched so tight around the pill his nails bit into his palm and stung.

Words won't fix this. Asher could deny everything Colton had said, but he wouldn't hear it, wouldn't believe him. It was partly the depression, flooding his brain and sending constant waves of black across every good thought. Some of it was the way he thought—the way life had taught him to think.

So he wouldn't try what he knew was useless.

Asher spun around and headed for the door.

Colton's legs twitched, but he controlled the impulse to run after Asher. His hands wanted to shake, so he wrapped them tighter around his upper arms. It was *good* Asher had listened to him. It had to be.

The rectangle of light from the doorway cut off. Asher was back with a paper cup from the bathroom, full of water.

Marching around the bed, he came to a stop just inches from Colton. "Here." The water cup was shoved at his hand. A trickle of it splashed out and left cold wetness across his skin. "And here. Today's just going to be one of the bad ones, and that's fine. At least give this one a chance to see if it's working." Asher waited until he unclenched his arms, then pressed the pill into his hand and watched until his fingers closed around it. He caressed the back of Colton's other hand until his tight fist relaxed, and set the paper cup into it.

Colton tried to deny how much he cherished even a small touch, but the leaping in his stomach made it so hard. He wanted Asher to touch him. He craved more of those embraces from yesterday. He didn't deserve such tender contact.

Everything I touch falls apart because I'm broken inside. The thought spiraled, repeating over and over, whether he wanted to hear it or not. There was no way for him to turn it off. Over the years he'd tried, and he'd learned the thoughts had a nasty, clingy life of their own. They would only leave when they were ready to.

"I gave it a chance." Instead of leaning closer, Colton stepped back. "I've been taking it regularly since January. I just forgot since I've been here." He scrubbed the fist, closed over the medicine, across his face and up to his eyes, winced at the scrape of stubble.

"Okay. Take it now, then, and we'll get you back on track tomorrow." Pure persistence was strong in Asher's voice. He stood there with his hands on his hips, the stubborn expression on his face making it clear he was ready to stand there as long as it took.

Yesterday those hips had been under his hands, smooth and damp. A little motor, running on guilt, twisted inside his guts. His mind whispered. *Broken. You break everything you touch.*

Colton gave up and swallowed the lamotrigine. He hadn't meant to forget, and the guilt of it added another layer to the heaviness pressing down on him. *This is definitely going to be one of the bad days.* The bed was beckoning, sending out irresistible nap rays. His eyes were gritty and wanted to close.

Asher stepped closer, lifting a hand to trace the rough stubble on his face. Colton flinched. Both of his hands came up to grasp Asher's wrist and make him stop.

"Asher, I meant it. You need someone like you, someone happy. Not me." Having to say it ripped something out of him.

With a soft laugh Asher leaned forward to rest his head on Colton's chest. His wrist was still caught between Colton's hands. "Too late. I want you. I don't need someone *normal*, Cole. Nothing you go through scares me away. I want to be there to help, as much as I can."

The words fell on his ears like rain, soaking into him softly. They were everything he wanted to hear. He let go of Asher's wrist, shoved at it, and twisted away. "It's never going away. I'll always be like this, exhausted and down in the dark." Real or imagined, he didn't know, but his head was whirling around in dizzy circles as if he was standing on the edge of some bottomless, black pit.

"Then I'll be in the dark with you." Asher reached out for his arm, so he stepped further back. "You know today is one of those days, but not every day is like this. It's hard to remember that, where you're at right now. I'll learn every idea that could help you, and we'll do it together. As much as I can, I'll be… your joy."

Colton crossed his arms, letting his fingers dig into the flesh. He welcomed the pain, dug in harder. No joy for him. Joy was for normal people, people who didn't carry around this monster on their backs all the time, this terrible dark weight.

More than anything he wanted to be asleep, not hearing the hope in Asher's voice. The sound of it cut right through him, made his heart twist. "No one can fix this, or *make* me be happy. It just doesn't work like that."

"Don't you think I know? After all these years watching you deal with it?" Asher rushed across the space between them and wrapped his arms around Colton, crossed arms and all. The shape of his body was becoming as familiar to Cole as the rumble of his voice already had been.

"I don't want to *make* you happy and I know I'm not a cure. I want to help you remember to do all the things to help keep you more even. The good healthy food and the walks outside and the medicine, and anything else we find. I want to be there for you, Cole. Don't push me out. Don't shove me away."

For one, glorious second he un-twisted his arms, let them come around Asher in return and crushed him to his chest. For a single, precious moment he let himself taste the sweetness of the hope Asher held out to him.

Even as Asher leaned into it, tiled his head up for a kiss, Colton was backing away.

Asher opened his arms and let go.

"You might mean it now, but after dealing with it for a few months this whole thing will get old. Believe me." No one deserved to be down with him in this dark.

"I mean it now, and I'll mean it in a few months. Believe me."

Even a small smile hurt. He shook his head and dropped onto the softness of his bed. With his eyes closed he shoved the pillow over his head and shut everything out.

Every tiny bit of light Asher shone at him punched a ragged hole that made him feel so much smaller, so much worse. He wished Asher would curl up in the bed next to him just as much as he hoped the other man would leave him alone. Then he felt guilty for wanting Asher's day to be ruined by holing up in this cave with him.

If he could just reach in and rip this part of him out, tear out the bit of his brain sending all of the heavy thoughts, he would do it in a heartbeat.

The door clicked shut softly behind Asher. Colton's nose itched and his eyes stung as they filled with tears of pain and relief.

CHAPTER SIX

Thursday morning Asher rolled out of bed and reached for his tennis shoes. Colton had tried to annoy him with running, but if it was the sort of thing he liked to do, then Asher could learn to tolerate it. A little exercise wouldn't kill him. The important thing was to get Cole out, moving around in the sunshine every day.

As he pulled on his sweats he pictured how good it was going to feel later when Colton peeled them back off. *We can disappear into the shower for a little while. Mom won't kick a fit. I think she knows I'm chasing after Cole.* He pulled on yesterday's shirt or tried to. He was in such a hurry he missed the armhole on the first try.

With a big, wide grin he sauntered down the hallway. After the briefest tap on the door he pushed it open. "Time to get up," he sang. "Let's go for one of your stupid runs."

Nothing.

His eyes adjusted to the dark room, enough to show him no one was on the bed. He stepped over and flung up the window shade, just like he had yesterday. No groan from the bed answered the slashing light. No cussing. Just a neat bed, in an empty room.

He took the steps downstairs two at a time, jumped the last couple to thump onto the floor at the bottom, and skidded into the kitchen.

"What on Earth?" Pam asked. The teapot was just starting to sing on the stove. "What's gotten into you this morning? Eggs and sausage, or just eggs?"

"Where's Colton?" he demanded.

"Colton? Upstairs." Shrugging, Pam reached for the egg carton.

"No, he's not. He's not there."

"Well, he's not downstairs. I've been up for almost fifteen minutes, and I haven't seen him."

Asher flung himself into a chair. "He left. He must have gotten up early and left."

Pam abandoned the eggs and came to sit next to him. "Why would he do that?"

He shifted his gaze over to examine her face and bit his lip. "I bet you have a pretty good idea why, Mom."

"You're chasing him down, and he doesn't want to be caught," she said, smiling.

"Pretty much. I'm not going to get into the gross details, but he wants to be caught. He wants it so much. But he keeps telling me I need to be with someone *normal*, someone who isn't messed up. Mom, he's so scared," Asher said. He leaned forward, cupping both hands behind his neck to try and scrub away some of the tension there. "I love him so much."

Her hand came to rest on his back and patted. "I know, baby." When he let his hands drop to his lap, her fingers rubbed the back of his neck soothingly. "What are you going to do?"

"Eat some eggs."

"Asher! It's not like you to give up." She stopped patting him. When he glanced at her, he saw she was frowning.

He let out a weak chuckle. "Eat some eggs and then go track his stupid ass down."

"Language," she warned.

Asher smiled. How many times had he heard her say the same thing, in the same tone, in this kitchen?

Leaning across his chair, he gave her a fierce, one-armed

hug. "I'm going to miss you when I'm in the dorms."

"You'll visit." She laughed. "Once a week when you need your laundry clean." She hugged him back. "I'll miss you, too, though."

Less than an hour later Asher opened the front door and froze.

Chris was standing on the doorstep with a hand still raised to knock. He looked so much like his son that Asher's poor heart leaped, but when he got to the frozen green of his hazel eyes the resemblance ended.

"Asher," Chris said, in stiff greeting. His hand dropped to his side. Asher saw the fingers flex, open and closed again.

"Chris."

Asher stood rigidly, waiting to hear why Chris had graced them with his presence today. His arm twitched towards the door, itching to close it in his face, but he had to go out if he wanted to get to his battered old *Tercel*. He could leave through the kitchen but then his mother would have to deal with the nasty little gnome decorating their front step.

"Where's Colton?" Chris finally asked.

Asher shut his eyes. *Fuck – I do not need this.* "I'm not sure. He's not here, though."

"I need to speak to him about our call yesterday, and he's not answering his phone. Are you sure he isn't here?" Chris craned his neck, trying to peer behind Asher.

"Colton left this morning," Asher said. He stepped forward, blocking more of the door. "Seriously, stop trying to get a look around me. It's rude."

Chris yanked his head back and turned a dark frown on Asher. "You've lied to me before. Forgive me if I don't believe you automatically."

Asher controlled the sneer trying to twist his lips sideways. "Fair enough. He's really not here, though. Are you going to go away, or do you want to search the house? I'd like to see your warrant."

The heavy, annoyed sigh was so familiar. Asher couldn't count the number of times he'd heard it. *What is this, like, flashback morning?* Asher remembered what it had been like when Chris lived here, too. He was like a drain, a huge, sucking hole that grabbed anything around him that wasn't *about him* and dragged it down into his own little drama. Everything always had to center on Chris. When it didn't, he had made them pay in a thousand little inventive ways. Disappointed sighing over Asher's attitude was only one of them. *Best thing Mom ever did, to divorce this idiot.*

"If you don't mind I'd like to come inside." Chris stepped forward, but Asher didn't move. He was within an inch of Chris's height now. He must have grown again in the year since they'd seen each other last.

"I do mind. Colton left, and I'm going to find him. Right now. I don't want to leave you alone with my mom, so I can't leave until you do. Are you going yet?"

"It's natural you should want to protect your mother," Chris said, in his stupid, fake understanding tone. Asher had always hated hearing it. "But the divorce has been final for a year and both of us have moved on, even if you haven't. I'm sure Pamela won't mind me looking upstairs and then leaving. I won't—Why would *you* need to find him?"

"Because he went without saying where he was going, or letting us know."

"Why would he?" Chris frowned again.

Asher released air in a steady stream, trying to control the impatient urge to shove past Chris and *go*. "Because I'm in love with him and he doesn't think he deserves it."

The man actually rocked back. He nearly fell off the front step but caught himself by windmilling his arms around. "In—love? With Colton? My son?" His lip twisted up as if he'd just smelled something unpleasant. "That's disgusting."

The doorframe bit into Asher's hand because he was squeezing it so hard. He caught his lip between his teeth, trying to keep in the hot words that wanted to fly out. The muscles in his neck tightened.

"Love is never disgusting."

Pam had come up behind them. Her voice was soft but firm. "Ten years ago I loved you. That wasn't disgusting, even though it did turn out to be a mistake." She stepped up behind Asher, forming a wall of solidarity.

Chris looked away. "Colton has had this crazy idea that he's been gay for years. Don't encourage it. You always give in to his little fits. You let him go on thinking these horrible things. If he'd just start taking some control over his life this wouldn't happen. It's your fault, both of you. You always—"

Asher felt the sting in his knuckles before he consciously realized his hand had formed itself into a fist and punched Chris. It hurt like a bitch, but he couldn't regret it, even as the older man crashed back onto the lawn. "You've been giving us those same tired old lines for years. Every psychiatrist you tried, every doctor, said the same thing. Colton has bipolar disorder. It's not all in his head. And neither is being gay. I'm sorry your church and your clients hate the sinner and love the sin or whatever, but we don't go to that church, and I don't really care."

His mother squeezed his shoulder. He lifted his still-throbbing hand to cover hers and give it a gentle pat.

Chris picked himself up, standing with jerky, awkward movements. His mouth was a wide, shocked O shape. Dead, yellow grass coated his impeccable, slate-gray sweater. A few pieces drifted off, floating away in the light breeze. Asher smirked.

"I'm never coming here again. And neither will my son. He can't be around you. You make him worse." He raised a hand to pat at the side of his face, gazing at Asher with a look rich with revulsion. "My behavior has always been above reproach, and my clients know that. The fact that you two are completely crazy is unfortunate, but they understand. I don't need to stand here listening to these lies. I'll never let him be in some sort of crazy *relationship* with you. It's disgusting, perverted—"

"Fuck off, Chris," Asher said. "It's not up to you anymore what Colton does or where he goes. And we'll always be here for him."

"I'm going to find him, right now. Don't follow me. Don't go near my son," Chris snarled.

Asher drew a deep, full breath and looked Chris right in his hard eyes. "He's only *your son* when you want something from him. The rest of the time you couldn't give a flying fuck what he wants or how he's doing. You've never been there for him with his problems, not once in his life. The only reason he thinks he's too broken to love is because *you* tell him he's broken, every time you see him." He dropped off of the step, walked closer.

Chris stepped back.

Blood pounded in Asher's head, blocking out everything but the man in front of him and the desire to beat him into the ground. "I'm not the disgusting person, Chris—you are."

Chris huffed. He turned on his heel and stalked back to the curb, where his black, sporty little *Honda* sat parked.

Asher watched until the engine had roared to life and Chris had peeled away. Then he turned around.

Pam was on the front step, frowning after her ex-husband. Her eyes shifted to glance at him. Slowly, the frown shifted to a wry, half-smile. "I wish you hadn't hit Chris, but I'm glad you did. He's wrong about Colton. Go find him. Before Chris does."

He grinned back at his mother. *Damn right I will.*

CHAPTER SEVEN

Heavy pounding on the door made Colton jump up out of his chair. Rubbing sweaty palms against the side of his jeans, he speed-walked across his tiny front room. If he took the time to get a drink and fix his dry throat, whoever was banging on his front door might go away. *Asher might go away.*

His heart was rabbiting around in his chest as he went to open it. *He's here! I knew it. I knew he'd come find me —*

The deadbolt clicked, louder than his heartbeat in his ears. He had to step back before the door hit him in the face.

"Asher, I told you —"

It wasn't Asher. His father stood in front of him, looking like a thundercloud all out of rain and ready to start on the lightning. *What have I done lately that pissed him off so bad?*

For several seconds, the only sound was Chris inhaling deeply through his nose. His mouth was working as if he were rehearsing which words to use.

Colton crossed his arms and lifted his chin waiting, watching. Was this, finally, the time for a showdown with Chris? It made him feel a little sick, knowing what he would have to say but… maybe it was time. Maybe it was past time to tell his father what he really thought of him.

Dried grass was stuck all over the arms of Chris's sweater, which was strange. His hazel eyes were a little wild, and he had a spot on the left side of his face. Something that looked like dirt smudged his cheekbone. *I might not be the only one with mental issues in this family.*

"So," Chris said.

Colton lifted one eyebrow. "So?"

"So this is where you're hiding, after your little fit at Pamela's house. Do you go there because you know they'll give into it? Is that why? I went over there to continue our discussion about paying for your tuition, and they didn't know where you were. It's irresponsible."

Colton's throat closed as all his muscled tightened. He cleared his throat and tried to clear his mind. He remembered from a self-help website. *When you have to deal with a narcissist, focus on one point and stick to that point, no matter how many distractions they throw out.* "This is my apartment, where I've lived for almost three years. It's on a public street, and you've had the address the whole time. I wouldn't call it *hiding.* Or irresponsible."

"You've hidden from everything all your life. It stops now. We're going back to Dr. Kilby at Behavioral Health. There has to be something he can diagnose." Chris shoved his hands into the pockets of his fashionable slacks. "I'll commit you myself. Until you can get your head right, there will be no more school. No more going over to see Pamela and no more Asher." His father's voice filled with thick, oily venom when he said Asher's name.

Colton leaned forward and narrowed his eyes. "No," he said.

"No?"

"No to all of that." *Pick your point and stick to it like glue.* "No, I'm not going to see Dr. Kilby again. No, I'm sure as hell not going to be committed. Dr. Kilby already diagnosed me. With *bi-polar-dis-order.*" He spaced the syllables out, slowly, as if talking to an infant.

Chris lifted his hand, trembling a little.

Colton's eyes widened. He braced himself, ready to intercept any movement the other man might make. His father had never hit him, not once in his life. He hoped he wasn't going to start now. "No. I'm not going to stay away from my stepmother, or Asher," Colton said.

Chris lowered his hand, stepped around him, and started to pace. "You left them today. Why can't you just stay away? Why can't you just be normal?" he pleaded.

"I left this morning because I needed a little time. It's not your business."

"It *is* my business when Asher has some psycho idea he's in *love* with you and you're going to have a *relationship* with him."

Colton's heart jumped and twisted. He couldn't stop the smile from spreading.

Chris must have seen the smile. He shook his head. "It's disgusting, and I will not have it. I told Asher that. I forbid him from going anywhere near you."

"When has Asher ever listened to you?" Colton wanted to know. He couldn't quite catch his breath. *He loves me, he really does, he told Dad about it, and that took some guts.* His heart was still singing buoyant, hopeful notes.

Chris stormed over to stand right in Colton's face. "You're not gay. There's nothing wrong with you! We just need to get you some—some help. Something."

"Like conversion therapy? Is that what you mean?" Colton shook his head, slowly.

"Is there a therapy for this? If it works, yes, that's what I mean." Chris put both hands on Colton's shoulders. His face was earnest. "Maybe it's just your-your bipolar thing. Disorder." It sounded like he could hardly get the word out. "It messes up your brain and makes you think gay. It's a delusion." He squeezed Colton, hard. "You're my son. I know you're normal. Somewhere in there is my little boy. I want him back."

Colton reached up and gently removed his father's hands.

"Besides the fact that it would lose you clients, I think it hurts you to imagine I could be so different from you. So you refuse to believe I could be."

"What? No, it's not—"

"I'm not finished, Dad." Colton stared at him, willing him to absorb the words for once. "Everything in your life is always concerning you. When Mom died, it was about you feeling better. When I was trying to figure out this bipolar thing, you needed it not to be true. Now it's true, but only because you can't stand to hear I'm gay. Dad, you're a selfish person."

Chris flinched away and turned his head. Colton got the impression he would have covered his ears like a child if the idea had occurred to him, but he wasn't finished.

"You need to accept how I am, or stay out of my way." His ultimatum, the first he'd ever given his father, rang into the silence. "I can't deal with this toxic drama coming up every time you remember I might not be an exact copy of you. I have other stuff to do, like finish college. Like have a life."

Nose flared, head lowered, Chris looked at him again. "What does that mean?"

Colton stood tall with his arms loose at his side and his chin up. The sweet current rushing through him felt a lot like freedom. "It means what I said exactly. Either accept me the way I am or leave me alone."

"You're not gay. I'm not, so how could you be?" his father insisted.

"If that's all you have to say, then the only choice is to leave me alone. Don't come over to see me. Don't call me. You're not a part of my life anymore." Lips pursed and head tilted to the side, Colton considered. "You barely were before."

Chris's eyes narrowed. "I'm not paying for your tuition.

Not another dime. Nothing, until you admit you're delusional and get yourself committed with Dr. Kilby like I said." He started toward the door and his typical grand, dramatic exit.

"Nope. Not going to," Colton said.

Chris swung back around. He looked like he couldn't believe what he was hearing.

Colton raised the volume of his voice a little. "If you go try to get me committed I'll get a voluntary assessment, prove I'm just fine, and file it with the police department, the hospital, and the campus. If you try anyway, I'll get a restraining order for harassment."

With one sharp shake of his head, Chris said, "You can have a few days to change your mind, to think about everything."

Colton lifted one shoulder in a shrug. His muscles smarted a little, where his father's grip had bitten into them. "Okay. Fine. Just know I won't change my mind. And don't come over here again. Don't call me. Just text. If I have time, I'll answer."

The sad thing was, his father literally wouldn't comprehend anything that went against his perfect reality. If it didn't fit in Chris's universe, he edited it out. A few minutes into his drive home, he would probably have rearranged this entire conversation in his head to make himself the good guy. It was a conversation Colton was going to have to repeat if he wanted his father to leave him alone.

His father nodded, stiffly. "I know you'll change your mind."

Colton shook his head. "You don't know anything. Don't hold your breath, Dad."

"Oh *please* go ahead and hold your breath," Asher said from the open doorway.

CHAPTER EIGHT

Chris spun around. Colton jumped.

Asher grinned at them. He leaned against the hard wooden frame and crossed one ankle loosely in front of the other. Closing the door had obviously taken second place to their nice, loud, argument. Fine with him.

"I told you to stay away from him!" Chris said.

"I don't actually give one shit," Asher replied. From across the room Colton smiled at him. His stomach did a flip-flop. "I just heard him tell you to leave."

Chris's head turned as he looked from Asher to Colton, back to Asher, once more at Colton, like he was watching a tennis match. Whatever he saw in their faces made him deflate, slumping his shoulders down. "A few days," he repeated. "You'll change your mind. You need help. You both need serious help." He sidled past Asher, leaning away so their bodies wouldn't touch.

Asher waited until the *thump-thump* of Chris going down the stairs had faded. "Are you going to tell me to leave, too? Going to tell me one more time you're no good for me?" he asked. He grabbed the doorknob in a death grip and squeezed, while the rest of him leaned forward as he waited for the answer.

"I can't," Colton said in a low voice. "I want what's best for you, but I want you more."

Finally! Asher's heart raced, his whole body filled with the sweet rush of victory.

He let go of the door and closed the distance between

them. His fingers twined through Colton's shaggy hair to tug his head down. Their lips crashed together. Asher let himself melt into the hard body while he worshiped Colton's gorgeous mouth with hot, greedy kisses. When he finally pulled back, he needed to gulp in air.

Colton lowered his forehead to rest against Asher's. "You're too stubborn." He sighed. "You always have been."

"I'm so proud of you," Asher said.

Colton's laugh brushed against his face, making him tingle. "What?"

"I'm proud of you. You did the right thing. He's not going to believe you for a long time, but you put up the first boundary. And I'll help you kick him back out every time he tries to come around." He watched Colton's expression, trying to gauge how stressed he was right now.

Colton squeezed his eyes shut and laughed a little. "And fill out all the paperwork? Because I think it might take some official paperwork to make him stop trying to *fix* me. He's been able to ignore the fact that I'm gay for so many years. Shoving it into his face now is obviously driving him nuts."

He opened his eyes again. Asher snatched a second to appreciate how much warmer the green seemed when it was Colton looking at him, not Chris.

He wrapped his arms a little tighter around Colton and shook him gently. "I could punch him again just for that. Stress is the *last* thing you need right now, but will he even consider it? Nope. Because he's more self-centered than a tornado. God forbid his clients ever find out about us, they'll freak the fuck out. Probably try to have us burned at the stake."

Colton let out a surprised grunt. "You hit him? That's what was on his face? I thought it was dirt. And burning people at the stake has been illegal for a long time in this country."

Asher laughed. "I said I loved you and he called me a disgusting pervert. It went downhill from there, and I ended up punching him."

The hand on his back froze. "You do?" Colton sounded hesitant.

Asher kissed the edge of his jaw, then the curve of his throat. "Of course I do. I've loved you forever." He snuck his hands under the edge of Colton's shirt to trace bare skin.

"You never said—"

"Well, we were stepbrothers, and then I was underage, and you weren't, and it was awkward." Asher tugged Colton's hips a little closer, so he could fit himself against Colton's erection. He closed his eyes and savored the heat. There had to be a way to continue this discussion in the little bedroom behind them.

"No, I mean this week. When we... talked about things."

He stopped trying to nudge Colton backward through the room. "I didn't?" Flipping through the week, he tried to remember their conversations. "No, I didn't. Shit."

Asher tilted his head so he could look Colton right in his stormy, still-sad eyes. "I love you, Colton. Everything about you. You're the strongest person I know. You're the best thing for me. My best choice. I'm going to help you get through all of this, with school and your medication and your dad, because I love you."

Colton's sigh filled the room. When he kissed Asher it went right to the soul, branding them together.

A tremor moved through him, making him shake. He'd just told Colton he loved him, and he wasn't trying to make Asher leave again. They were kissing. No arguing or persuading—they were meshed together, gasping, taking, giving. Maybe Colton actually believed him. Maybe his plan had worked.

"I still think you could do better... " Colton jerked and

trailed off when Asher bit the side of his neck. He lifted a shoulder to rub over the spot and grinned at Asher.

"There isn't any *better* than you, Colton." Asher kissed him, hard. He yanked his shirt off and reached out to pull on Colton's. Eager, shaky, he dove onto his chest as soon as it was bare, catching a nipple between his lips.

Colton's breath hissed between his teeth.

Anticipation streaked through Asher, lighting up his whole body.

Colton's hands framed his face and lifted with gentle insistence. "I love you, too," he said. His eyes were firm on Asher's. His face was open and sincere. "I have for so long, and I couldn't stay away from you, even when I tried. I love you. I want you here with me through all of this shit, even though I hate dragging you along." He leaned forward for a deep, soft kiss.

"Don't. I want to be here," Asher said when he had his breath back. His heart was still leaping around after hearing the words he'd wanted to hear so badly, for so long. He kissed Colton again, opening for him with a little moan, not caring how desperate he might look.

He was already unsnapping his jeans as they made it to the bedroom, still kissing. Colton's head banged into his while he worked on his own jeans, and he laughed. Asher barely registered the thump.

Their pants ended up in a heap on the floor, boxers on top of them. Out in the open, his erection throbbed, begging for attention.

Colton pressed him back on the bed. A soft, fluffy comforter caressed his back. Asher groaned as his cock was covered with wet heat. The tip of Colton's tongue grazed his tip, and his hips shot off the bed. The thrill of it went through him, need streaking along his skin from top to bottom. He was leaking already, blown into little pieces by how good it felt, how in love he was with the man pleasuring him right now.

If Colton didn't stop sucking him he was going to come, so hard. With a small twist he bucked a little, getting the idea across, and when Colton sat up, Asher leaned forward to press him back onto the bed where he had been a second ago.

"Let me," he said.

"I love you," Colton said again. The smile on his face was brilliant — the brightest Asher had ever seen him.

He took his time, exploring the whole thick, smooth length of him until Colton was panting and gripping the bed. Asher moaned around his cock and tried to take him deeper. It had been a while. He was shaking, trying to hold himself back. And that was Colton's strong hand, digging into the blue comforter to drag it up in bunches. Colton's body, quivering under him. The cock he had snuck peeks at for years, stretching his lips. A lot of dreams were coming true.

He was dizzy with greed when Colton pushed his shoulders back, wound so tight he might explode.

"I have to be inside you. Right now." Colton sounded fevered, impatient.

As if he had to ask. Asher fell backward onto the bed, holding his legs open. Every inch of him throbbed and strained for contact.

Colton flung himself sideways. He fished a little tube and the foil square of a condom out of the cheap plastic drawer by the bed. "You need to be opened?"

Asher shook his head. "Just get over here. I need you so bad." Next time he could help Colton spread the lube on. He'd enjoy it just as much as he was enjoying watching Colton sheath himself and get the condom nice and slippery right now.

In spite of what he'd said, Colton went slowly going in, stretching him inch by torturous inch. A cry ripped out of Asher's throat. Colton grabbed both of Asher's arms and swept them up over his head, pinning him as he sank in deeper. He worked Asher's nipples with his mouth. Asher was out of his mind, flying high on the pleasure.

They were both sweating already, sliding together as if they had always been together like this. Colton finally let go of Asher's arms, and he used the freedom to grip his thick, dark hair. His mouth was so hungry on Asher's that he was afraid of falling in and drowning. At least he'd die happy.

Colton's breath huffed out as he snapped his hips, going hard and deep. Asher wrapped his arms around Colton's neck. His body was so tight that Asher knew he had to be close, so he reached in between them to grab his cock and stroke.

"Now," Colton panted. "Now." His teeth closed over the slope of Asher's shoulder as he pulsed inside of him. A gasp tore out of him as the orgasm ripped through him and left him reeling. Above him, inside him, Colton trembled.

Asher didn't want to move, not an inch. He'd happily stay here all day on this tiny twin mattress, Colton's ragged breaths in his ear, sweat sticking their bodies together. Beard stubble scraped his face when Colton rested his cheek against Asher's.

"Shit," Cole breathed.

Asher nodded and let his head drop back onto the pillow. His heart had slowed down and the sweat was drying on his temples by the time Colton pulled out and rolled off to the side to dispose of the condom. When Asher turned over to face him Colton was still smiling.

"I love you," Asher said again.

Colton closed his eyes, and his mouth worked, trying to decide between the smile and a frown. "I don't know why."

Asher smacked his chest lightly. "Don't start. I'll list every reason and stick it in a frame for you to look at. I'm not changing my mind, and you aren't chasing me off."

Colton snorted. "I know how stubborn you are." He leaned forward to wrap an arm around Asher and tug him close. "Don't leave me," he said into Asher's neck. "I'll do my best to deal with everything if you just stay."

Asher traced his thumb along the firm jaw, pressed a soft kiss to Colton's lips. "I'm not going anywhere."

Colton kissed him back, licking across his closed lips, coaxing him open. Every worry drained away, every problem faded for those few seconds, leaving Asher filled with pure, shiny happiness.

Asher leaned back a little, stretched out his legs. The blanket seemed so far away, but the sweat drying on his body was chilly. "Except to the dorms." He tried to grip the fuzzy cotton with his toes to drag it up. It slid away, so he reached again.

"What?" Colton leaned over, absently, and snagged the blanket causing Asher so much trouble.

"I said, I'm not going anywhere, except to the dorms. No offense, but I'm a little too young to move in with someone yet. And my room is all set up already. Maybe next year."

Colton grinned and smoothed the covers over both of them. "The dorms are just a few blocks away from here. I can come get you every morning for our jog."

Asher covered his eyes with his hands and groaned.

Chapter Nine

"Are you sure that's everything?" Pam asked. She had two plastic shopping bags draped over each arm and a pillow caught between her elbow and body. Early morning light streamed over everything, already taking the nip out of the air.

Colton nodded.

"I'm sure." Asher looked over at Colton and rolled his eyes, but the smile he wore was soft. His own arms were full of three cardboard boxes, with a set of sheets plunked on top.

"Let me get those," Colton offered again. It was almost too warm for the thick blue sweatshirt he wore, but the breeze was still chilly. He compromised by rolling the sleeves up, while Pam locked her car.

Pam smiled at him and shook her head. "Nothing else is going to fit on top of the suitcase you've got, Cole. Go on. We'll fill up the whole elevator." They crossed the parking lot together, a jumble of bags and boxes accompanied by the rumble of plastic wheels. "I don't see why we couldn't make two trips."

"Because I can do it in one," Asher said.

"We," Pam corrected.

"Yeah, we can do it. In one trip."

By the time he'd gotten out of the elevator and down the hallway to room 110, Colton's shoulder was sore from maneuvering the giant suitcase and keeping the smaller one from falling off the top of it. He wrinkled his nose as they passed the big communal shower room. The antiseptic bleach smell coming out of it filled up the hallway in a solid block.

"Here," Asher's voice urged from behind him. He stepped aside to let Asher fumble with the doorknob.

As soon as he was inside he tugged the small case off of the bigger one and tossed it on the bed. Pam set down her bags and bustled around behind them, opening the blinds, checking the light switch, while Asher opened and inspected the standing wardrobe.

"You've got the money on your meal card?" she asked finally.

"I checked yesterday, and it was there," Asher reassured her.

"I've got your schedule, so if you text me when you're supposed to be in class, I'll know," she said. Colton thought her voice sounded more *wobbly* than *warning*.

Asher smiled, the same big, innocent smile he'd used on Colton a week ago after chucking a pillow at his head. "I'll be in class. Not texting." He mimed crossing his heart.

"I'm not making your bed," Pam announced. "You can do that yourself. But I'll see you on Saturday for dinner?"

Colton caught the shine of tears in her eyes, under the bright, fluorescent light. He walked over to drape one arm around her.

She leaned into him and sniffled. "You, too, Cole."

He squeezed her. "For sure. I'll be there right after I get off work."

Asher came over to hug her from the other side. "I'll be there. Love you, Mom."

"I love you, too, baby. I'll let you get settled in," she said. They both hugged her one more time before she turned to leave. At the doorway she turned around to smile at Colton. "Take care of him."

"I will," he said and meant it.

She smiled and left.

Colton's muscles jumped as Asher's arms wrapped around him from behind. "You will?" Asher asked. "You're not going to change your mind and try to get me to leave for my own good again?"

He turned around to wrap Asher up in a tight hold. "I thought about it. But no, I won't try again." When he looked down, Asher's smile had new, sly edges.

"I should make the bed since my mom made it pretty clear she won't," Asher said.

"I'll help." Colton started to release him and step back, but Asher's hands dipped down into his back pockets. His breath came out in a huff when Asher pulled him forward. "But first... " he said and lifted his head to press their lips together.

They kissed until Colton's heart was thundering and he couldn't remember if the door was open or shut. Asher's hands were distracting, squeezing him through his pockets. He cupped a hand around Asher's neck, anchoring him so he could nibble along his jawline.

"We should christen the bed," Asher said.

"No. Asher, no. Your roommate could get here any time." In spite of what he said, his hands were creeping under Asher's shirt, finding the smooth, warm skin to touch.

"Then we'd better hurry." Asher reached down to rub him lightly through the front of his jeans.

Colton started shrugging off his sweatshirt. "Lock the door. What are we supposed to say if he shows up early and he's standing out there knocking?"

Asher obeyed, tugging on the handle to make sure the door was firmly shut. He pulled off his own shirt as he walked back over to join Colton. "We'll tell him you're my big brother and you're allowed up here."

Colton paused in the middle of tugging down his jeans. "I am *not* your big brother. That would make this erection, the one right here"—he pointed to the obvious bulge tenting the front of his boxers—"creepy and wrong. I'm just the son of the guy your mom—"

"—used to be married to. I know." Asher laughed.

Colton looked at the man walking towards him—the hard chest roped with muscle, the narrow hips he couldn't wait to get a grip on, that shining blond hair. Male perfection. Pure, bright joy. *All mine.*

As soon as Asher was close enough, he tugged him over to give him a good, hard kiss. "God, I love you," Colton said.

Asher kissed him back. "I love you, too. I always will."

Colton hit the pillow as he tumbled onto the bed. He grabbed Asher to drag him down, too. *I believe you.* His heart was swollen full, achy with love. "We can take a run tomorrow," he said.

Asher laughed. "Or we could do this instead. This is the way I like to exercise."

"Maybe," Colton agreed and drew Asher's head down for another kiss.

The End

ABOUT THE AUTHOR

Lili Draguer is an author and fan of erotic romance. She loves watching romantic comedies, the sappier the better, snarky banter a definite plus. When she's not running around after her three kids, opening doors for the cat overlord, or hanging out with the husband she's writing love stories that slip into the super sexy and forbidden. If you can't get enough of steamy sparks that lead to a happily ever after (no cheating!) these books are for you.

In the first book of the Taboo Love series, teacher and student discover why staying after school can be a Big Mistake —

... Mr. Smith demanded, "What's going on here?"

"I-I was just—I left something—" David stuttered.

Mr. Smith interrupted, "In Mrs. Pinelli's office? In the girls' locker room? I doubt it. Right now, it is definitely not school hours. So you should not *be* at school. Go home, Mr. Cruz."

David spluttered out a few more excuses, but he slunk away without trying to argue any further. Was he imagining it? Or did David look—relieved? Mr. Smith watched with his arms folded across his chest and thick brows pulled down, until David was gone. What had David been coming in here to do? It was obvious it had something to do with Carolyn's office, since the rest of the locker room was visible and very empty. But what?

Her office should have been locked right now. It was true that she was out and about more than in the office, shouting students into action on the field or in the gym. She was notorious for forgetting to lock her office door. He rolled his eyes, thinking of the gossip. *Wasn't it last year one of the students had stashed a stolen laptop in her desk?* It had been pure luck that it had been found.

Had David been trying to steal something? Hide something? Meet someone to do whatever weird thing teenagers could be up to, at night, in an empty school? He snorted as he walked over to try getting in to the office. It was so late, his time would be better spent locking up and going home. But he did have a responsibility to make sure nothing had been secreted away in his co-worker's office. The old-fashioned brass doorknob was cold, smooth against his palm as he turned it, opened the door and stepped through.

The transition from faint gloom to pitch dark left him blinking back temporary blindness. He jumped when someone grabbed his wrist and dragged him in.

The click of the lock was loud behind him as he was propelled towards the one hard-backed chair in the room. It hit the back of his knees, and he was so stunned he let himself sit down. He tried to force his eyes to adjust. The barest trace of light snuck in where the thick metal door met the floor. It wasn't enough.

When he opened his mouth to roar for an explanation, soft lips covered his in a kiss. *What the hell?*

Weight came to rest in his lap and he realized that it was a person, along with the discovery that the person was an exceptional kisser.

Who-what in the hell?

Whoever it was rubbed against him as they shifted to reach for the buttons on his shirt. His body reacted instantly, without his approval, coming to attention.

This could be anyone! Why did the thought excite him? It should have horrified him.

As the soft mouth released his he drew in a deep breath, to shout . . .

Their love is off limits, for so many reasons.

Planning a sexy surprise for her boyfriend one night, Jenny Carter doesn't double check who she just grabbed in the dark, and in one big mistake ends up seducing her high school Math teacher, Mr. Smith. Trying to deny the out of bounds attraction she just sparked between them turns out to be futile. The consequences for being caught would destroy their lives. Teacher and student will have to decide what to do about their intense and forbidden romance, and the love growing wild in their hearts. Conventional wisdom says that if you love something you should let it go, but nothing about their love is conventional.